Jesus' Christmas Party

NICHOLAS ALLAN

RED FOX

For Richard McBrien

JESUS' CHRISTMAS PARTY

A RED FOX BOOK 978 1 782 95589 4

First published in Great Britain by Hutchinson,
an imprint of Random House Children's Publishers UK
A Random House Group Company

Hutchinson edition published 1991
Red Fox edition published 1996, 2004
This edition published 2011

7 9 10 8

Copyright © Nicholas Allan, 1991

The right of Nicholas Allan to be identified as the author of this work has been asserted
in accordance with the Copyright, Designs and Patents Act 1988.

Red Fox Books are published by Random House Children's Publishers UK
61–63 Uxbridge Road, London W5 5SA

www.randomhousechildrens.co.uk
www.randomhouse.co.uk
www.nicholasallan.co.uk

Addresses for companies within The Random House Group Limited can be found at:
www.randomhouse.co.uk/offices.htm

THE RANDOM HOUSE GROUP Limited Reg. No. 954009

A CIP catalogue record for this book is available from the British Library.

Printed in China

An entertaining musical adaption of this story, written by Roger Parsley and suitable
for school or church nativity use, is available from Starshine Music.
Tel. +44 (0) 1323 764 334
Full details can be found at www.starshine.co.uk

There was nothing the innkeeper liked
more than a good night's sleep.

But that night there was
a knock at the door.

'No room,' said the innkeeper.
'But we're tired and have travelled
  through night and day.'
'There's only the stable round the back.
  Here's two blankets. Sign the register.'
So they signed it: 'Mary and Joseph.'

Then he shut the door,
climbed the stairs,
got into bed,
and went to sleep.

But then, later, there was
another knock at the door.

'Excuse me. I wonder if
you could lend us
another, smaller blanket?'

'There. One smaller blanket,'
said the innkeeper.

Then he shut the door,
climbed the stairs,
got into bed,
and went to sleep.

But then a bright light
woke him up.

'That's *all* I need,'
said the innkeeper.

Then he shut the door,
climbed the stairs,
drew the curtains,
got into bed,
and went to sleep.

But then there was *another*
knock at the door.

'We are three shepherds.'
'Well, what's the matter? Lost your sheep?'
'We've come to see Mary and Joseph.'
'ROUND THE BACK,'
 said the innkeeper.

Then he shut the door,
climbed the stairs,
got into bed,
and went to sleep.

But then there was yet
another knock at the door.

'We are three kings. We've come—'

'ROUND THE BACK!'

He slammed the door,
climbed the stairs,
got into bed,
and went to sleep.

But *then* a chorus of
singing woke him up.

'RIGHT – THAT DOES IT!'

So he got out of bed,

stomped down the stairs,

threw open the door,

went round the back,
stormed into the stable,
and was just about
to speak when –

'Ssshh!' whispered everybody.
'You'll wake the baby!'

'*Baby?*' said the innkeeper.

'Yes, a baby has this night been born.'

'Oh?' said the innkeeper,
looking crossly into the manger.

And just at that moment, suddenly,
amazingly, his anger seemed to fly away.
'Oh,' said the innkeeper, 'isn't he *lovely*!'

In fact, he thought he was so special,
he woke up *all* the guests at the inn,

so that they could come and have
a look at the baby too.

So no one got much
sleep that night!